SCH BERT

FANTASIE IN F MINOR

OPUS 103; D. 940
FOR ONE PIANO, FOUR HANDS

EDITED BY MAURICE HINSON AND ALLISON NELSON

AN ALFRED MASTERWORK EDITION

Alfred Music Publishing Co., Inc.
P.O. Box 10003
Van Nuys, CA 91410-0003
alfred.com

ISBN-10: 0-7390-7911-5
ISBN-13: 978-0-7390-7911-9

FRANZ SCHUBERT

FANTASIE IN F MINOR, OP. 103; D. 940 (FOR ONE PIANO, FOUR HANDS)

Edited by Maurice Hinson and Allison Nelson

Foreword

Franz Schubert (1797–1828) began composing the *Fantasie in F Minor*, Op. 103, in January of 1828 and completed it in April of that year, just a few months before his premature death. The *Fantasie* was dedicated to one of his favorite students, Karoline Esterhazy. It is probably Schubert's most-often performed piano duet, and it is filled with some of his loveliest and most enticing melodies. Schubert kept the theme in its original form throughout the work, in contrast to Franz Liszt (1811–1886), who, in compositions of similar construction, varied the theme each time it appeared. Furthermore, inspiration from the Baroque and Classical periods—French overture style, decorative ornamentation, scherzo and trio form, fugal writing—take precedence over compositional innovations of the Romantic period.

ABOUT THE MUSIC

This work is one of the great masterpieces of the piano duet repertoire, as well as being recognized as one of Schubert's finest works. It is written in a free but well-defined four-section cycle similar to a sonata.

Form: **A** = measures 1–23; **A**¹ = 23–36; **A** = 37–47; **B** = 48–90; **A** = 91–102; transition to *Largo* = 102–120.

The *Fantasie* begins with a rather serious melody. It opens in minor but soon moves to a cheerful major mood. This opening theme should not be hurried. Taking plenty of time is necessary to play the sixteenth followed by the grace note in measures 2–4 of the Primo and similar places.

Form: **A** = measures 121–133; **B** = 133–149; **A** = 149–163.

The *Largo* opens in the unexpected key of F-sharp minor. It is dramatic, and a dotted rhythm in French overture style is used to create tension. However, in measures 134–148, a lovely romantic melody needing a complete change of sound and mood is introduced.

Form: **A** = measures 164–198; **A**¹ = 199–249; **A** = 250–274; trio = 274–314; **A** = 314–348; **A**¹ = 349–399; **A** = 400–426; transition to *Tempo I* = 426–439.

The *Allegro vivace* is a fun, lively scherzo, which reflects Schubert's lighthearted sense of humor. Very little pedal is needed, and clear staccatos and separations are in order. A *con delicatezza* trio-like section appears in measures 274–314.

Form: **A** (from the first section) = measures 440–475; **B** (fugue based on mm. 48–90 of the first section) = 476–556; **A** (coda) = 557–572.

The fugue in the *Tempo I* moves forward with great excitement. (In fact, Schubert had indicated *più mosso* at the beginning of the fugue, but this notation was later marked through.) While the tempo remains steady throughout, the texture builds. The use of a triplet accompaniment in the Secondo part leads to an exciting climax. This forward motion is interrupted by a sudden and dramatic measure of silence, which is followed by a brief return to the opening melody in the coda. The work concludes with a progression of chords including extraordinary harmonic changes in measure 569.

ABOUT THIS EDITION

Metronome Markings: One of the most important elements in achieving a convincing interpretation of the *Fantasie* is finding a satisfactory tempo. If played too fast, it loses its special intimate character and becomes superficial. If played too slowly, it loses its forward motion and becomes tedious and cumbersome. The metronome markings are suggestions from the editors. Each section has its own personality, and metronome markings can be adjusted by the performers to find the "just right" tempos. The interpretation should be elegant and, at times, emotionally moving.

Pedal: Although no pedaling is indicated in this edition, the work requires tasteful pedaling. It should be done by the Primo player. The pedal should be used throughout as needed without blurring the sound.

Fingering: All fingering in this edition is editorial. In several passages, the physical discomfort for the Secondo can be eliminated by playing the first notes of the measure as an octave in the left hand (measures 126 and 127, for instance).

Articulations and Ornaments: Staccato and phrase markings are inconsistent throughout the original edition, but there are enough to establish a pattern of non legato in each section. Minor notational inconsistencies have been corrected in this edition. Trills and inverted mordents begin on the principal note. The *acciaccaturas* found in the opening measures of the Primo and used throughout this work are "crushed notes" to be played a split-second before the principal note and released immediately.

SOURCES CONSULTED

Dale, Kathleen. *Nineteenth Century Piano Music*. London, Oxford University Press, 1954.

Einstein, Alfred. *Schubert*. London, Cassell & Co. Ltd.,1951.

Lubin, Ernest. *The Piano Duet*. New York, Grossman Publishers, 1970.

McGraw, Cameron. *Piano Duet Repertoire*. Bloomington, Indiana University Press, 1981.

Weekley, Dallas and Nancy Arganbright. *Schubert's Music for Piano Four-Hands*. White Plains, NY, Pro/Am Music Resources, Inc., 1990.

Fantasie

SECONDO

Franz Schubert (1797–1828)
Op. 103

Fantasie

PRIMO

Franz Schubert (1797–1828)
Op. 103

Allegro molto moderato (♩ = 100)

SECONDO